I Do Not Like Greens!

Parent's Introduction

Welcome to **We Read Phonics**! This series is designed to help you assist your child in reading. Each book includes a story, as well as some simple word games to play with your child. The games focus on the phonics skills and sight words your child will use in reading the story.

Here are some recommendations for using this book with your child:

1 Word Play

There are word games both before and after the story. Make these games fun and playful. If your child becomes bored or frustrated, play a different game or take a break.

Can you think of a word that rhymes with cake?

Bake!

Phonics is a method of sounding out words by blending together letter sounds. However, not all words can be "sounded out." **Sight words** are frequently used words that usually cannot be sounded out.

2 Read the Story

After some word play, read the story aloud to your child—or read the story together, by reading aloud at the same time or by taking turns. As you and your child read, move your finger under the words.

Next, have your child read the entire story to you while you follow along with your finger under the words. If there is some difficulty with a word, either help your child to sound it out or wait about five seconds and then say the word.

3 Discuss and Read Again

After reading the story, talk about it with your child. Ask questions like, "What happened in the story?" and "What was the best part?" It will be helpful for your child to read this story to you several times. Another great way for your child to practice is by reading the book to a younger sibling, a pet, or even a stuffed animal!

Now you can read the story to me!

LEVEL 4 **Level 4** introduces words with long "e," "o," and "u" (as in *Pete, nose,* and *flute*) and the long "e" sound made with the vowel pairs "ee" and "ea." It also introduces the soft "c" and "g" sounds (as in *nice* and *cage*), and "or" (as in *sports*).

I Do Not Like Greens!

A We Read Phonics™ Book
Level 4

Text Copyright © 2010 by Treasure Bay, Inc.
Illustrations Copyright © 2010 by Jeffrey Ebbeler

Reading Consultants: Bruce Johnson, M.Ed., and Dorothy Taguchi, Ph.D.

We Read Phonics™ is a trademark of Treasure Bay, Inc.

Published by
Treasure Bay, Inc.
P.O. Box 119
Novato, CA 94948 USA

Printed in Singapore

Library of Congress Catalog Card Number: 2010921692

Hardcover ISBN-13: 978-1-60115-331-9
Paperback ISBN-13: 978-1-60115-332-6

We Read Phonics™
Patent Pending

Visit us online at:
www.TreasureBayBooks.com

PR 07/10

I Do Not Like Greens!

By Paul Orshoski

Illustrated by Jeffrey Ebbeler

Making Words

Creating words using certain letters will help your child read this story.

Materials: thick paper or cardboard; pencil, crayon, or marker; scissors

1 Cut 2 x 2 inch squares from the paper or cardboard and print these letters and letter combinations on the squares: ea, ee, b, t, s, p, l, m, n, and w.

2 Place the cards letter side up in front of your child.

3 Ask your child to make and say words using the letters available. For example, your child could choose the letters "b," "ee," and "t," and make the word *beet.*

4 If your child has difficulty, try presenting letters that will make a specific word. For example, present "b," "ea," and "n," and ask your child to make *bean.* You could then ask your child to find a letter to change the word to *lean.*

5 Ask your child to make as many words as possible that use the "ea" and "ee" cards. These letter patterns are used in the story. Possible words include *meals, eat, peas, peels, meat, beets, steam, sweet, beans, seem, leans,* and *seat.*

Sight Word Game

Word Bingo

This is a fun way to practice recognizing some sight words used in the story.

Materials: 3 x 5 inch cards; paper or cardboard; pencils, crayons, or markers; ruler; scissors

1. Write each word listed on the right on a 3 x 5 inch card.

2. Then create some Bingo cards with your child. Each player can make his own card.

3. Start by making a 4 by 4 or 5 by 5 grid. Fill the grid with random words from the list. Words can be used more than once. (See example in illustration above.)

4. Create some colored dots to put over the words.

5. Mix the word cards and place them face down. A player turns over a card and reads the word.

6. Players put a dot on the words on their Bingo card if matched. If the word appears more than once on a card, put a dot on each one.

7. The first player to complete a row, across, up and down, or diagonally, wins the game.

8. Play again!

from

two

give

comes

would

old

who

one

out

My dad likes to bake.
No junk for my meals!

He makes me eat fish sticks
with peas that he peels.

I ask for red meat
with a good bit of fat.

Yet he hands me red beets
that I slip to the cat.

He stuffs me with bran
and puts rice in my face.

If I do not eat it,
he gets on my case.

He steams up fresh green beans...

...he hopes I will like.

He feeds me small seeds . . .

...that I send on a hike.

Here comes a radish
he cleans with a hose . . .

. . . and two bite-size carrots
I stick in my nose.

Dad treats me to salads
as green as the frogs,...

...but I would much rather
eat ribs and hot dogs.

I have to munch greens
or I take the heat...

...not like his old dog,
who is huge in the seat.

Dad fills her with treats,
as she sits on her throne.

And one time each week
he will toss me a bone.

She pigs out on chips
and big chunks of meat.

She gulps lots of fat
and snacks that are sweet.

That junk makes her sick
and makes her so weak...

…but with all my greens,
I run like a streak.

Phonics Game

Guess the Word

This is a fun way to practice blending letter sounds together, which helps children learn to read new words.

SSS...eee...d...zzz.

Seeds!

1. Choose a simple word in the story that can be sounded out. Say the sound for each letter in the word. For example, for the word *jeans*, say the sounds for the letters "j," long "e" (as in *seat*), "n," and "s," with a slight pause between the sounds.

2. Ask your child to guess or say the word.

3. If your child does not reply correctly, then repeat and extend the sounds. If your child continues to have difficulty, run the sounds closer and closer together.

4. Continue with additional words from the story, such as *junk, meat, beets, rice, beans, seeds, grease,* and *chips*.

5. For variation, let your child provide the prompt sounds to you.

Phonics Game

Make a Face

Help your child practice some of the words in the story.

Materials: paper; pencil, crayon, or marker

1. Choose one of the words from this list: *beets, hands, rice, fresh, lemon, rather, treat, sweet, streak.*

2. At the bottom of the paper, draw a line for each letter in the word. For example, if the word is *treat*, draw five lines, creating a spot for each letter.

3. The child guesses a letter. If the letter is in the chosen word, put the letter on the appropriate line. For example, if the word is *treat* and the child guesses the letter "t," put the letter "t" in the first and fifth spots. If the letter is not in the chosen word, start to draw a face. Start with a circle for the basic face, then the eyes, then eyebrows, and so on.

4. The object of the game is for the child to guess the correct letters and the word before the face is completed. If your child has trouble, give hints, such as: "Guess the letter that makes the sound *rrrr.*"

5. Play again with another word.

If you liked *I Do Not Like Greens!*,
here is another **We Read Phonics** book you are sure to enjoy!

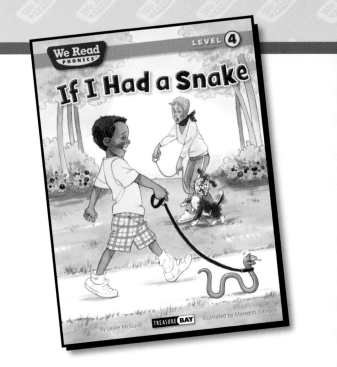

If I Had a Snake

Bruce wants a snake—a nice green snake. A snake would be so much fun! Bruce thinks about all the things he would do with his snake. He would make a big cage for the snake, feed him ice cream, and take him to class. There is just one little problem. Will his mom let him get a snake?